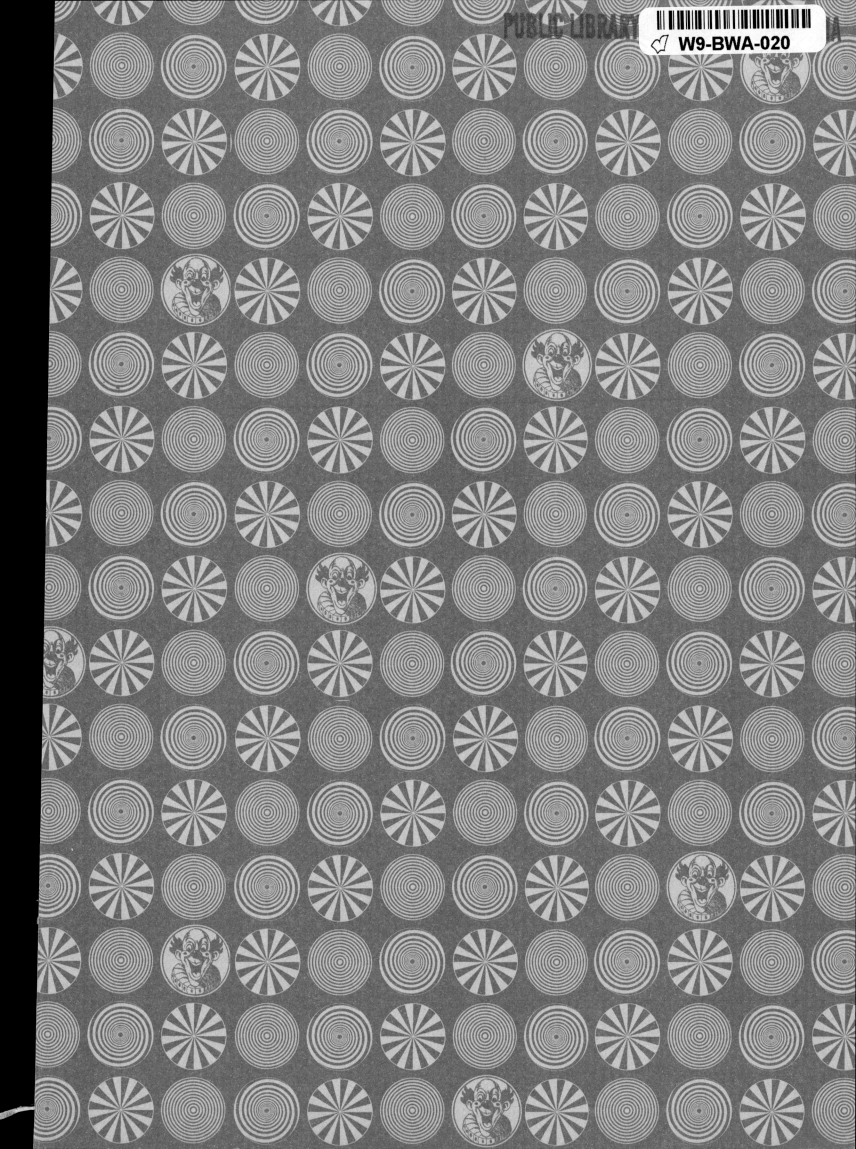

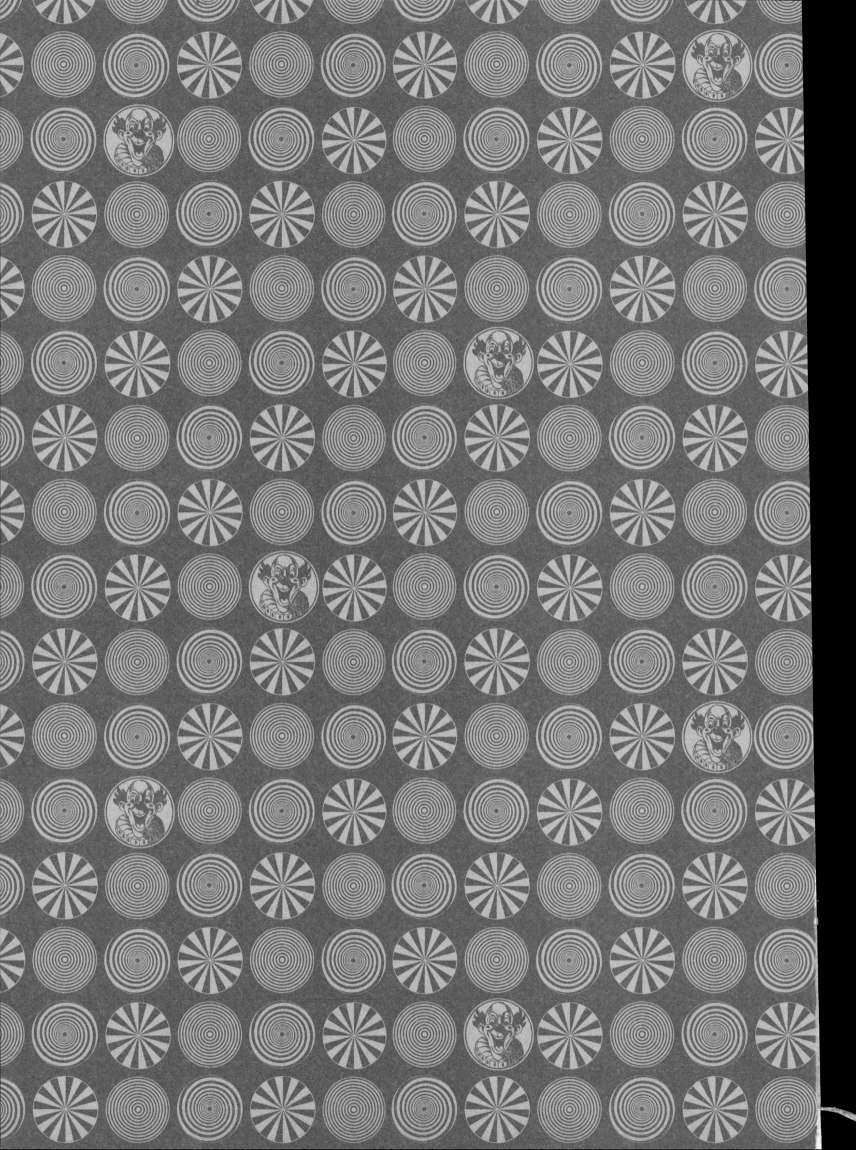

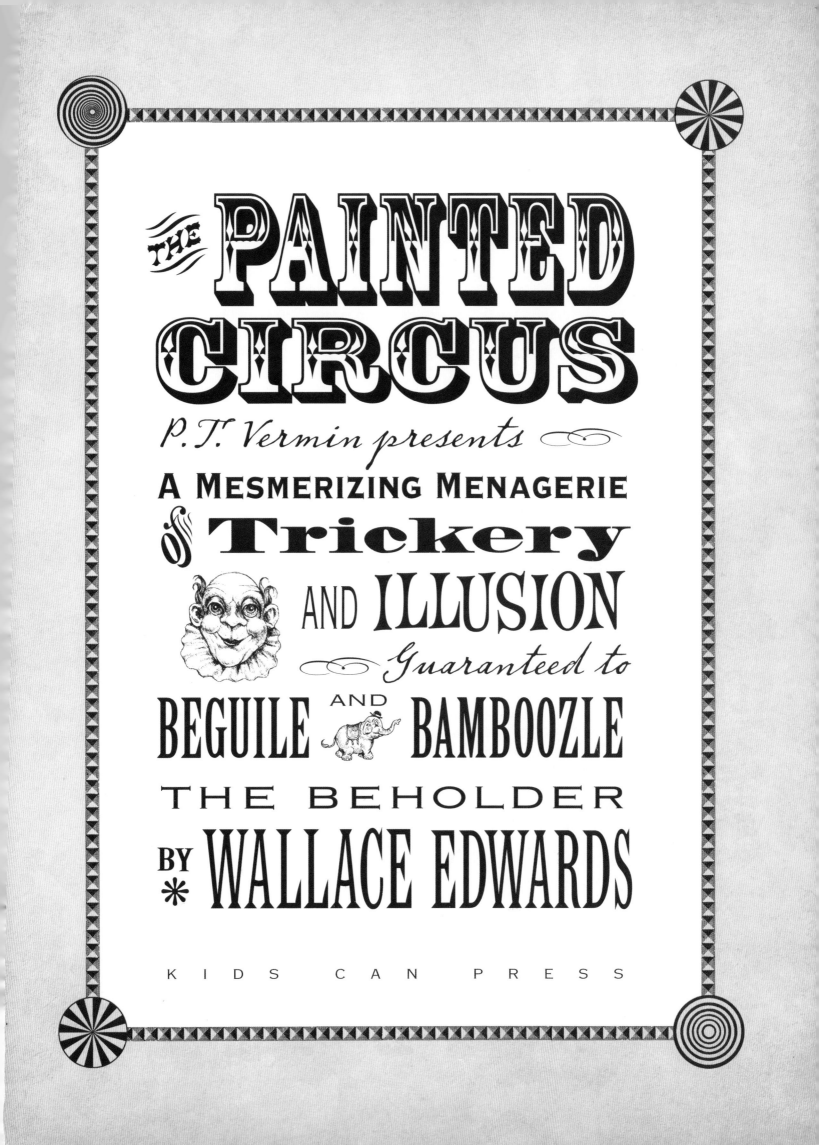

THE PAINTED CIRCUS

P.T. Vermin presents

A MESMERIZING MENAGERIE
of **Trickery** AND ILLUSION
Guaranteed to
BEGUILE AND BAMBOOZLE
THE BEHOLDER
BY ✳ WALLACE EDWARDS

KIDS CAN PRESS

For Katie, my love,
and Harriet, Stella Charles,
George, Sadie, Calla,
Matthew and Jane — W.E.

Text and illustrations © 2007 Wallace Edwards

Kids Can Press acknowledges the financial support of the Government of Ontario, through the Ontario Media Development Corporation's Ontario Book Initiative; the Ontario Arts Council; the Canada Council for the Arts; and the Government of Canada, through the BPIDP, for our publishing activity.

Published in Canada by   Published in the U.S. by
Kids Can Press Ltd.   Kids Can Press Ltd.
29 Birch Avenue   2250 Military Road
Toronto, ON M4V 1E2   Tonawanda, NY 14150

www.kidscanpress.com

The paintings in this book were rendered in watercolor, colored pencil and gouache. The line drawings were rendered in pen and ink.

Edited by Tara Walker
Designed by Karen Powers
Printed and bound in China

This book is smyth sewn casebound.

CM 07 0 9 8 7 6 5 4 3 2 1

LIBRARY AND ARCHIVES CANADA CATALOGUING IN PUBLICATION

Edwards, Wallace
The painted circus: P.T. Vermin presents a mesmerizing menagerie of trickery and illusion guaranteed to beguile and bamboozle the beholder / by Wallace Edwards.

ISBN 978-1-55337-720-7 (bound)

I. Title.

PS8559.D88P35 2007   jC843'.6   C2007-900894-1

Kids Can Press is a *Corus*™ Entertainment company

STEP RIGHT UP!

Hurry, hurry! Step right up! And behold, within this colossal canvas,
a parade of performances that will puzzle the peepers,
a myriad of marvelous merriments that will mystify the mind
and acts of astonishing artistry that will arrest the imagination!

UNDER THE BIG TOP

Ladies and gentlemen! Hold onto your hats, heels, wigs and lollipops!
For I, P.T. VERMIN, ringmouse extraordinaire, am about to take you on
a magical tour of visual trickery and optical illusions. I bring you
the greatest show in the galaxy – I bring you THE PAINTED CIRCUS!
{And if you're truly bamboozled, all mysteries will be revealed after the grand finale!}

SPINNING WHEELS

Thrill to the high-speed antics of ZIPPY THE ZEBRA RACER and his swift and silly sidekicks! CAN YOU MAKE THEIR WHEELS SPIN?

{*Move the book in small, quick circles.*}

Pirate Parrots

Cast your eyes upon WINKIN, BLINKIN and CHUCKLES, three plundering pirates transformed into parrots by island magic of long ago. USE *YOUR* MAGIC TO SEE THE PARROTS BECOME PIRATES. CAN YOU TELL WHICH IS WHICH?

{Turn the book upside down.}

KING & QUEEN OF HEARTS

Be charmed by the GREEN KING as he shows his heart to his lady fair.
WILL SHE REVEAL HER HEART IN RETURN?
{*Stare at the dot on the king's heart for twenty seconds,
then look at the queen's card for her answer.*}

LESTER THE JESTER

Look way, way up, high above the crowd, and laugh as LESTER THE JESTER perches precariously on a pole! WHICH FACE ON HIS FOLDED CARD POPS FORWARD? WHAT HAPPENS TO THE FACES WHEN YOU TURN THEM UPSIDE DOWN?

THE BUTTERFLY BOX

Behold a magical metamorphosis!
Caterpillars crawl in the box and beautiful butterflies emerge!
DO YOU NOTICE SOMETHING ODD ABOUT THE BOX?
CAN YOU FIND TWO HIDDEN CLOWN FACES? A TIGER'S FACE? MORE?

THE SPECTRAL SPHERE

Observe DAISY, a dragon of distinction, as she dazzles us with her
dynamic display of sphere-handling skills. Daisy is balancing a red-and-yellow ball,
but she's also hiding an orange one. CAN YOU MAKE HER ORANGE BALL APPEAR?
{*Move the book in small, quick circles while staring at the ball on her head.*}

THE ENCHANTED CANDLE

Gasp in awe at the pyrotechnic pageantry of PROFESSOR F.E. LINE
as he conjures a creature of the night with his enchanted candle!
WHAT SORT OF CREATURE DOES HIS SHADOW TURN INTO?
{*Close one eye and tilt the book away from you to find out.*}

THE LAUGHING CLOWN

Alas, his trumpet is twisted so he will not smile. GRIMLY, the fantastical clown of renown, needs some cheer. CAN YOU MAKE HIM LAUGH?

{*Make your funniest face and move back from the book.*}

THE PERILOUS & PERPLEXING PLATFORM

Delight at the dramatic and daring dance moves of ISADORA DUMPTY
(sister of the famous Dave Dumpty) atop a perilous platform!
WHICH CROSSBAR ON HER PLATFORM LOOKS LONGER? TOP OR BOTTOM?

Norwegian Marching Ducks

Look to the heavens and witness the brawn and balance of
BOYD TUMBLES as he turns himself into a living bridge for the famous
NORWEGIAN MARCHING DUCKS! DO YOU SEE ALL SEVEN DUCKS?

CRYPTIC CUBES

Be spellbound by the stupendous strength of Rhino Boy
BUNNY THUMBMUSCLE. HOW MANY CUBES IS HE HOLDING ALOFT?
{*Some say six. Some say seven. What say you?*}

THE DISAPPEARING RABBIT

Gadzooks! The melancholy magician has lost his rabbit
and the crowd is in an uproar! CAN YOU HELP HIM
FIND HIS RABBIT AND MAKE EVERYONE HAPPY AGAIN?
{*Turn the book upside down.*}

BELLY OF WONDERS

Stare if you dare at EL PORKO, the mysterious tattooed enigma!
WHAT STRANGE SIGHTS APPEAR ON HIS BELLY OF WONDERS?
{*Choose the black or green face on the banner and stare at it
for twenty seconds, then look at the pig's belly.*}

THE PHANTOM STILT

He's part Dutch, part Spanish and a tad Polish. He's ODATA, a teetering, tottering, two-toed toad! CAN YOU MAKE HIS OTHER STILT APPEAR? {*Lift the book so it's horizontal and the right corner is resting against the tip of your nose. Then stare with both eyes at the shoe and look up the stilt toward the toad.*}

THE MAGIC WAND

DR. TERRY UR needs some help fending off a flurry of flying ice-cream cones!
CAN YOU FIX HIS MAGIC WAND AND MAKE THE FLYING CONE DISAPPEAR?
{Hold the book away from you. Then close your right eye and, while
staring at the dog, bring the book slowly toward you.}

The Flying Fishtastics

Jump for joy at the astounding acrobatics of the FLYING FISHTASTICS!
One leaps through the hoop; one leaps past.
WHICH IS WHICH? CAN YOU MAKE THEM SWITCH?

GYMNASTIC GIANTS OF THE JUNGLE

Regard the grandeur and grace of these GYMNASTIC GIANTS OF THE JUNGLE
as they balance and bend into a wheel of elegant elephants.
HOW MANY ELEPHANTS DO YOU SEE?

TREAT FOR TWO

It's feeding time for the CANDY GATORS. One candy, two ravenous reptiles!
CAN YOU HELP THEM SHARE THE JELLY BEAN?
*{While staring at the red jelly bean with both eyes, slowly bring the book
toward your face until your nose covers the jelly bean.}*

FRAIDY CAT

Sing along with the fabled FRAIDY CAT as she shrieks a song to soothe herself.
HAS SHE PUT SOMEONE TO SLEEP WITH HER CURIOUS CROONING?
{*Turn the book upside down to find out and to see something happen to the spider.*}

MASHED-POTATO MARKSMAN

Step back! Or be struck by a mushy missile as the magnificent mashed-potato marksman SPUDS GALORE attempts to hit a bull's-eye with his terrifying over-the-shoulder technique. HAS HE HIT THE EYE, OR MADE ONE?

{*Move back from the book and look at the potato-covered screen. See anything?*}

THE DANCER WITH SIX FACES

Be amazed by the twists, turns and sundry windings of WIGGLES O'SHAY,
the high-steppingest, hat-kickingest dancing fool that ever was!
DO YOU SEE WHY HE IS KNOWN AS "THE DANCER WITH SIX FACES"?
{*Look at the empty spaces around his body.*}

THE TOSS-UP

Nearly last, but not least, all the way from the dark depths of the Sargasso Sea, it's SID THE SQUID, the gigantic gelatinous juggler! HOW MANY STEPS LEAD UP TO SID?

And, finally, the moment you've all been waiting for ...
It's time for me, P.T. VERMIN, to get into the act.
Up, up, up with EVERYTHING!

THE GRAND FINALE

It's all in the air now, AROUND AND AROUND AND DOWN AND DOWN …

… AND INTO THE HAT.

Thus concludes our humble entertainment.
WHAT'S UNDER *YOUR* HAT?

MYSTERIES REVEALED

SPINNING WHEELS:
If you quickly move the book in small circles, the wheels will appear to spin around.

PIRATE PARROTS:
When the book is turned upside down, you will see three pirate heads. The pirate on the left is Winkin, the pirate in the middle is Chuckles and the pirate on the right is Blinkin.

KING & QUEEN OF HEARTS:
If you stare at the king's green heart, a red heart will appear on the queen's card. So, yes, she reveals her heart in return!

LESTER THE JESTER:
Both faces will pop forward, depending on your perspective. One face will appear to pop forward at first. But if you continue to stare at the card, you will see the fold a different way: the same face will retreat and the other face will pop forward. Also, if you turn the book upside down, the smiley face turns into a frowning face and vice versa.

THE BUTTERFLY BOX:
The box is an impossible object: the opening on the right appears further forward or further back, depending on how you look at it. If you look at the wings of the three big butterflies, you will see clown faces in two of them and an upside-down tiger's face in the third.

THE SPECTRAL SPHERE:
If you quickly move the book in small circles while staring at the ball on Daisy's head, you will see a smaller orange ball appear inside the other.

THE ENCHANTED CANDLE:
When you close one eye and tilt the book away from you, you will see the wizard's shadow take the shape of a cat.

THE LAUGHING CLOWN:
If you stand back from the book, the clown will appear to laugh.

THE PERILOUS & PERPLEXING PLATFORM:
The top crossbar appears longer, but they are actually both exactly the same length!

NORWEGIAN MARCHING DUCKS:
If you turn the book on its side, you will see the seventh duck. Boyd's heel is the tip of its bill and his collar is its tail.

CRYPTIC CUBES:
If you see the black sides as the *tops* of the cubes, you will count six cubes. If you see the black sides as the *bottoms* of the cubes, you will count seven.

THE DISAPPEARING RABBIT:
When the book is turned upside down, the rabbit appears in the magician's hat! At the same time, the crowd's frowns turn into smiles.

BELLY OF WONDERS:
If you stare at the black face, you will see the same face in white on El Porko's belly. If you stare at the green face, you will see the same face in red.

THE PHANTOM STILT:
When you stare at the shoe and look up the stilt as the book rests against the tip of your nose, another stilt will appear.

THE MAGIC WAND:
If you bring the book slowly toward you while closing your right eye and staring at the dog, the ice-cream cone will disappear.

THE FLYING FISHTASTICS:
Both fish appear to leap through the hoop and past it, depending on your perspective. If you see the red fish jumping through the hoop, the blue fish will appear to leap past. If you see the blue fish jumping through the hoop, the red fish will appear to leap past.

GYMNASTIC GIANTS OF THE JUNGLE:
There are nine elephant bodies in the picture, but only seven heads!

TREAT FOR TWO:
If you stare at the jelly bean while slowly bringing the book toward you until your nose covers the bean, both gators will appear to eat the candy.

FRAIDY CAT:
When the book is turned upside down, the Fraidy Cat becomes a sleeping lion – and the spider becomes a spider *monkey*!

MASHED-POTATO MARKSMAN:
When you move back from the book, you will see an eye in the mashed-potato-covered screen.

THE DANCER WITH SIX FACES:
If you look closely, you will see five faces in the empty spaces around the dancer. Five faces plus the dancer's own face equals six faces!

THE TOSS-UP:
There are three steps on one side of the platform and four on the other.

P.S. Did you notice the trick at the top corner of each page? If you flip the left pages while looking at the elephant in the top corner, you will see him tipping his top hat. If you flip the right pages while looking at the face in that corner, you will see a queen's face spin around and turn into a king!

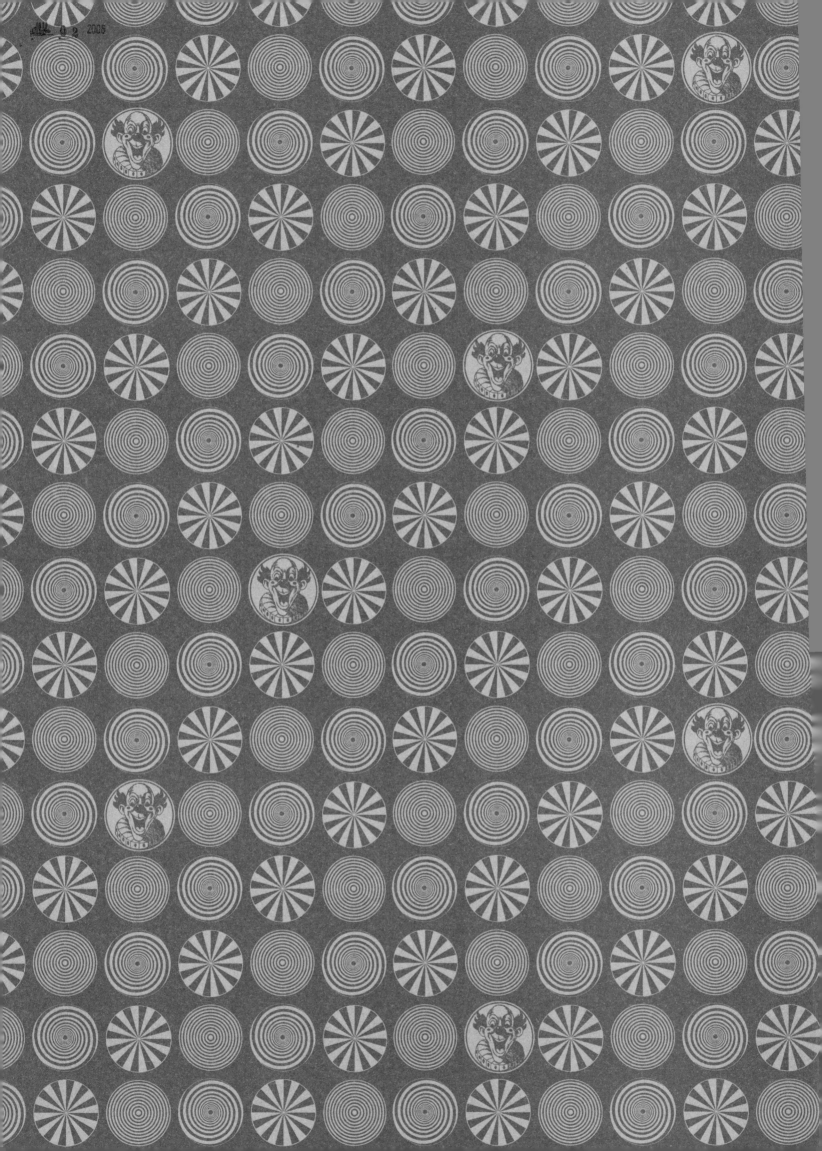